The Hummingbirds
Have Acquired a Taste for Blood

The Hummingbirds
Have Acquired a Taste for Blood

Poems and Pictures
Too Creepy for the Classroom

Sage Rooker and RK Rugg

Tree-Lion Press

Tree-Lion Press

Purveyors of Particularly Audacious Ideas

This is a work of fiction. Names, places, characters and incidents
are products of the author's imagination or are used fictitiously and
are not to be construed as real. Any resemblance to actual events,
locales, organizations or persons, living or dead,
is entirely coincidental.

Design and illustration by RK Rugg

Library of Congress Control Number: 2024917121

ISBN (paperback): 979-8-9886993-3-0

For the students
--past, present and future--
of Room #221B

And yet again, for IAK

The teller of supernatural tales
should be well frightened in the telling...

—Edith Wharton

Contents

Late at Night, A Pantoum

Late at night
Sick for sleep
Comes the fright
Black so deep

Sick for sleep
Sounds. The wall
Black so deep
Sounds. The hall

Sounds the wall
Whispers, moans
Sounds the hall
Clattering bones

Whispers moans
call my name
Clattering bones
do the same

Call my name
Bring the fright
Still the same
Late at night.

~

Granite Tears on Halloween

Granite Tears on Halloween

In our youthful quest for treats, perhaps we've lingered
too late
In this part of town, this once-rich neighborhood in
decline
Where the decaying mansions all have stone lions at the
gates
And rock walls crumble, heavy with sullen ivy on the
vine.

We should have bypassed
    this once-rich neighborhood in decline,
But here we are nonetheless in the small hours of
    Halloween night,
Making our way along rock walls heavy with ivy on the
    vine,
A watching, waiting vegetation that denies the moon's
    wan light.

Lost in revelry, we creep through the small hours of
    Halloween night,
Nagging misgivings pushed aside, climbing the walk to
    ring the bell,
Skirting the forbidding vegetation by the moon's wan
    light.
And heartily, warily asserting that surely, surely all will
    be well,

Pushing our misgivings aside as we climb the walk to
    ring the bell.
But wait. Look there. Why does the petrified guardian
    weep?
What has he seen? What does he know? Surely all
    would be well
If only the feline sentry would relax, if only he would
    sleep.

But oh, the petrified guardian does weep.
And oh, we have lingered far too late.
The feline sentry will find no comfort, will find no
    sleep.
Pray, now pity us. And pity the stone lion at the gate.

~

Bruh-ugh.

The big green bug from outer space
crash-landed in the yard.
Perhaps it meant to find that place;
It didn't land too hard.

It hit the grass and dug a hole.
It burrowed in the ground.
And then at night, away it stole
and didn't make a sound.

Unlucky milkman on his rounds
was first to see the beast.
Unlucky milkman...crunching sounds;
a xeno-insect feast.

The gardener and the paper boy,
they followed soon right after.
Yummy breakfast. Insect joy
and squeaky insect laughter.

With tummy full, and quite content,
the bug now settled down,
remembered now why it was sent
and why it came to town.

It plodded on through August heat
until it found the school.
It plodded on with all six feet.
The gym was nice and cool.

The students out for summer break;
one custodian on site.
The bug ate till it couldn't take
another bitsy bite.

The creepy bug, on all six legs
found where they kept the gear
for games and sports. It laid its eggs
right there. And there. And here

Among the nets and basketballs
the racquets and the hoops.
Near hockey pucks and volleyballs
and jump-ropes all in loops.

Now that its job was finally done,
the bug went back outside.
Beneath the sweltering summer sun,
it curled up tight and died.

But it left behind a big old batch
of babies down the hall,
round insect eggs all set to hatch
when kids come back in fall.

So when you go to gym this year...
and see a 'ball' that's new?
You'll know that there's a bug egg here,
you'll know just what to do.

Run.

~

The Little Ghost Who Could

Once a little ghostly girl

Found that she couldn't scare.

No matter how she'd wisp and whirl,

She couldn't raise a hair.

She couldn't give the shivers

And she couldn't goose a bump.

When it came to causing quivers,

She was in an awful slump.

She went to Haunting School

And she studied there quite hard.

Her teacher was a master ghoul

Who was held in high regard.

She learned to moan and wail

And she learned a hearty "Boo!"

She pulled a black cat's tail;

Knocked pictures all askew.

She finally earned her G.E.D.
(for Ghostly Education).
She laughed and laughed with ghastly glee
Upon her graduation.

Now she's the best there ever was.
The ghosts all know her name.
Scaring's all she ever does.
She's in the hall of fame.

So if you ever sense a chill
Or hear whispers in the wood,
You may have just been haunted
By the little ghost who could!

~

iRobbie

Cleaner 'bot at work.

Disposes of the body

Then returns to its charging station.

~

fingernails on hardwood

$f$ingernails on hardwood

something unseen

skitters down the hallway

~

Moonlit Ivory

Moonlit ivory
In the graveyard of legend
zombies have weapons

~

I Hear Sounds / In This Old House

I hear sounds in the walls of this old house
    when it's late at night,
oh so faintly. A whisper, a moan, a sigh in the
    dark. There's
a presence that waits, existing behind the
    panels, out of sight;
An entity devoid of compassion and foreign to
    hopes and prayers.

Oh so faintly, it whispers, it moans, it sighs in
    the dark as if there's
no question that the crevices and crannies and
    crawlspaces are its own.
An entity devoid of compassion and foreign to
    hopes and prayers,
it's neither plant nor animal, it lacks leaf, root,
    blood, skin and bone.

There's no question that the crevices and
    crannies and crawlspaces are its own—
This fungal intruder, this ancient malignancy,
    with its spores for seeds
is neither plant nor animal, lacking leaves, roots,
    blood, skin or bone.
And yet, hidden in the still and quiet and
    undisturbed places of my home, it feeds.

This fungal intruder, this ancient malignancy,
    with its spores for seeds,
it grows and consumes, it thrives on decay.
    Darkness is what allows it to be.
Hidden in the still and quiet and undisturbed
    places of my home, it feeds.
But when it becomes hungry, when it needs
    more darkness—will it come for me?

It grows and consumes, it thrives on decay.
    Darkness is what allows it to be
a presence that waits, existing behind the
    panels, out of sight.
But now it is hungry. It needs more darkness.
    And it comes for me.
I hear its sounds in the walls of this old house
    tonight.

~

Ghostly Trio I: One-Liners

A Tooth in the Stew

Not my own.

Blood is Thicker than Water

It spreads much better on toast.

Graveyard Dirt

Be sure to wash behind your ears.

~

In Eastern Massachusetts

In eastern Massachusetts

there's a cemetery around every corner.
Pockets of manicured landscapes
or overgrown patches of headstones.
They catch you by surprise.
Historical and very picturesque,
each an oasis of calm among the stifling crowds
of buildings, cars, trees.

But I no longer go out running after dark.

~

Vegetative Unrest in Southern Mexico:
A Villanelle

The residents of Tuxtla stay out of the little
    park
just off *Libramiento Norte* when they can,
    but especially at night.
"Not a good place to be when it's dark."

Trees with sly leaves and sullen bark,
relentless undergrowth, all brambles that
    scratch and fight.
The residents of Tuxtla stay out of the little
    park,

wary of a place that bears no urban mark,
accepts no rumble of traffic, refuses the
    glow of streetlight.
"Not a good place to be when it's dark."

A brooding and woods-choked pocket, it
    stands in stark
contrast to the docile buildings grown up
    around the site.
The residents of Tuxtla stay out of the little
    park,

heeding *las historias de sus abuelos,* the
    ones that hark
back to great-grandparents' nighttime fright.
"Not a good place to be when it's dark."

Civilization grinds forth; ruler and monarch
    believe the wilds are retreated before
    their might.
But still, the people who live here stay out of
    the park
and know it's not a good place to be when
    it's dark.

~

Summer School I:
Spider in the Gym

Watching a spider drag its prey
across the gym floor at summer school
at the junior high

makes me wonder just what happened here.
I can't imagine the spider had a web
out in the middle of the basketball court—
I mean, it's all flat, nothing to connect to,
to stretch the web between, you know?

Maybe it fell from the ceiling?
Maybe it caught a fly up there in a web
in the gym rafters and spun it
all up in silk and then...what?
Both fell down somehow to the floor below?

Well, whatever happened, there it is.
The spider—not a big one—inching along
the hardwood,
making its way toward the safety
of the darkness beneath
the folded-up bleachers,
the housefly dragging about three inches
behind.

The teacher has some of the kids playing
dodgeball (mostly the guys).
I'm just hanging out on the side,
waiting for P.E. to end, waiting
to go back to the classroom.

Whenever the kids
run by this side of the court,
the spider pauses. Stops in its trek. Stops in
its tracks.
Then begins again.

Six yards to go. Then pause. Then five.
Like a Fremen crossing the sandy dunes of
Arrakis.

As the dodgeball war rages, all it would take
would be
one step in this direction on the part
of the pursuers or the pursued,
one errant bounce in this direction on the
part of their red rubber missiles,
to end the spider's efforts
forever.

What must we—the students, the teachers,
the humans—appear as
from the arachnidial perspective?
Booming, looming mountains that approach
and recede
with hurtling speed and no reason or logic.
Monsters the size and disposition of
elemental forces of nature,
unknowable entities that crash and slam and
then
pound away into the unfathomable distance.

Stepping softly,
I take two paces
and position myself
between the spider
and the activity

on the court beyond.

~

"Love is in the Stars"

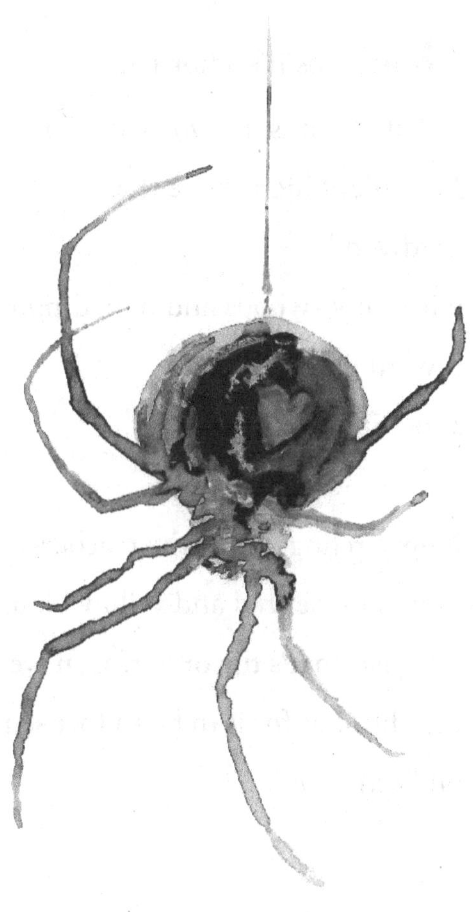

~

Summer School II:
Wasp in the Gym

Or perhaps it's a hornet.

Whatever it is, it's got a stinger.

Lazy flight high above the

hardwood

with slow swoops and now dipping

toward us as we play

a modified version of tag.

Now circling one of the teachers,

drawn by her red and yellow blouse

(at least, that's the only reason we

can think of for it to be so focused

on her.)

I grab a discarded grey hoodie and

knock it to the ground.

And step on it.

A disconcertingly loud

and solid crunch beneath my sneaker.

The rest of the kids cheer. The

teachers smile and relax.

Until a few minutes later, when

the next sinister insect buzzes down

from the ceiling, thin of waist,

black and yellow markings a wordless

warning: Beware! Danger! Go Away!

The next day, the custodians shut

us out of the gym, doors locked.

The teachers take us to a

vacant classroom and we play boardgames.

~

A Vampire Lives in my Attic

A vampire lives in my attic.

No one believes me, but he's there.

The first time I saw him was when my mom had me go up there, up the pull-out ladder to get the box of fall decorations that we keep shoved out of sight, up under the eaves.. Things for Halloween and Thanksgiving and stuff.

It's dark and shadowy, even when the one lone lightbulb is lit. He was over in the far corner, standing there with his big black cape and big white fangs. When he realized that I had seen him, he suddenly changed himself into dust motes and faded away into the gloom.

When I told my mom about it, she just laughed and said, "Oh, my, I guess you've got the spooky season on your mind already!"

My big sister laughed, too. When I tried to tell her that I was really serious, that I had really seen a vampire in the attic, she just laughed harder. And now she likes to jump out at me from behind corners and yell "Boo!" Or sneak up behind me and grab me and whisper, "I *vant* to *suck* your *BLOOD!*"

The vampire must have found out that
no one thinks I'm telling the truth, because
now he doesn't even try to keep out of sight or
hide from me. When I take my clothes down to
the laundry room in the basement, there he is,
glaring at me from under the stairs. When I
wake up in the middle of the night to go to the
bathroom, I see him peering at me from around
the corner down at the end of the hall. When
I'm trying to fall asleep, I hear his leathery
bat-wings fluttering in my closet.

Last night when I came home from the movies,
he was perched up on the top of my house and
he even gave me the "I've-got-my-eyes-on-you"
gesture (you know, the one where someone
makes a 'V' with their fingers, points them at
their own eyes and then points them at you).
I was so scared! But by the time I could poke my
sister and stammer, "V-v-v-vampire!" he had
already turned into a bat and flown away.

I'm getting more and more worried about what
comes next.

A vampire lives in my attic.

And no one believes me that he's there...

~

Ghostly Trio II: Limericks

In my closet there's an old skeleton.

It's been there since I was just nine or ten.

I ask it each night,

"Can you give me a fright?"

And it answers each time, "Oh, how well I can!"

In a house on the edge of the swamp

Where the ogres and trolls like to romp

Lives a witch all alone

Except for a bone

Which she keeps there to chew on and chomp.

Once was a werewolf in full o' moon

then human again in the sun o' noon.

Because of the light

In daytime or night

He knew that a change would be comin' soon.

~

They Say At This Time of Year

They Say At This Time of Year

They say at this time of year a gate opens
to let ghosts and goblins come through.
Thinking on this, you imagine shrieks
and creaks as the portal swings wide
on rusty hinges that call out into the night.
But you're just as much a child
as those trick-or-treaters who come to your door
begging sweets in exchange for not pranking you.

The veil to the land of the dead parts not with a
    sound
but with a smell.
And now you call to mind the stench
of decay, of corruption, of rotting meat
but you're wrong again.
You've been too far removed
from the farm and village life.
Hollywood has trained you to think in tropes.

They knew about it, though, back in the long ago,
about the earthy pungent smell of
smouldering vegetation
that accompanied the glow of the will-o-the-wisp.
They put candles and coals
inside of
turnips and gourds.
Because they knew.

Think about that when you're eating the leftover
    candy
at the bottom of the bowl at the end of the night
and you go to blow out the flame
in your jack-o-lantern
 and you become aware of the scent of
singed pumpkin.
Think about it.
And lock the door.
You know. Just in case.

~

Clowns

Clowns are crazy.

Clowns are freaks.

Clowns will pinch your rosy cheeks.

Big red lips

And pale white faces.

Springing out from hidden places.

On a bike

Or in a car,

Clowns from near and clowns from far.

Scary clowns

March one-by-one.

Whoever thought that this was fun?

Creepy eyebrows

All a-wiggle.

Creepy laughter when they giggle.

Some honk a horn
While others mime,
Planning evil all the time.

Dead, flat eyes
Behind their smile,
Plotting evil all the while.

Giant shoes
And ruffled collar
This one's short, and that one's taller.

Run and hide
From the clown
When the circus comes to town!

~

Beware the Black-Eyed Child, My Dear

Away back in the Pennsylvania hill country, where knowledge passes down from generation to generation, there's one bit of advice that goes unquestioned... to beware the Black-Eyed Child.

There's usually someone in any given family who can recall an eerie encounter with a pale and lonely waif out in the nighttime where no little child should have been. They describe a youngster with an unsettling air and large eyes, all taken up with pupil until nary a sliver of white remains.

And everyone knows someone—or knows someone who knows someone—who has gone missing in the dark.

You'll not find this piece of regional lore written down anywhere, and you won't hear it shared outside of the close-knit rural communities. But those who have grown up in the area know the lines by heart, and they, in turn, pass them down to their own children...

Beware the Black-Eyed Child, my dear.
Avoid the mineshafts at dark, my dear.
Stray not too far from your home at night.
And lest you draw the Child's attention, dear,
Whistle not in the moon's full light.

Best beware the Black-Eyed child.
Neither the pets nor the livestock are safe, my
    dear,
not when a Black-Eyed Child knows thirst.
Dusk to the witching hour, my dear,
be aware of the times that are worst.

Beware the Black-Eyed Child, my dear.
Best latch the windows and lock the doors and
    best close the gates to the barn.
Best be at home with a fire, sleep tight
and then best of all is to wake with the morn.

Best beware the Black-Eyed child.
Stay out of the woods at dark, my dear.
Stay close to your house at night.
Beware the Black-Eyed Child,
my dear.

Best beware
of the Black-Eyed
Child.

~

The Autumn Forest

The autumn forest
Striding among the pine trees
I am so alone

~

Stopping by the
Zombie Club table
during fall registration

Yeah, naw, just looking, thanks.

But, I mean, do you have a pamphlet or something?

'Cuz, like, how's it work, you know? I mean, do you eat my brain, and then I'm a zombie, or what?

'Cuz I'm getting kinda tired, you know? Tired of taking all the precautions.

Tired of having to watch out for you guys when I'm on a walk, making sure I cross the street if I see you coming, working hard to keep a safe distance away from you.

Tired of not being able to just go out for dinner, or go to a concert, or hang out in the park with friends. It wears you down, man.

And I see all the others who have just gone ahead and become zombies

and I'm like, "Wow, it must be nice to be so carefree. They're just going along and nothing bothers them, just shuffling and shambling, lah-dee-dah."

I'm so tired. You know?

Sure, man, you can have my number, go ahead and get in touch. You know.

~

Bones

I.

I went to the dentist today. They took x-rays of my mouth and put the pictures up on a computer screen on the wall. And it struck me...teeth are like *bones*.

Teeth are like bones that *actually stick out of our bodies.*

Teeth are like bones that actually stick out of our bodies, *covered up by the skin of our face, until we choose to open up that skin and expose these bits of bone to the world.*

If you really think about it, it's almost like our teeth are retractable, like Wolverine's claws or something, the way we can hide them just by keeping our lips closed over them and then— Snap! We reveal them and take a bite out of something.

And that all got me to thinking about the other bones in our bodies.

All those bones are all covered up by our skin, right?

But then *inside* the bones, *inside* the skull, is our *brain.*

And the brain is where we really are,
right? I mean, you could lose all of your
other body parts, but as long as your
brain was still okay, you'd still be *you*, right?

And so, if that's the case, that we—you and me,
our actual identities—are in the brain, then that
means that we—you and me—are being carried
around inside a shell of bone that is all wrapped
up inside a casing of skin.

I'll tell you what else I got to thinking; I think
I'm gonna stop arguing with my Mom when she
tells me to put on my helmet when I go out
riding on my bike.

II.

So, yeah. Bones, right? Bones and skeletons.

My aunt and uncle went to France a few years
ago, and one place they visited was the
catacombs. Back in the 1700s, the cemeteries in
Paris were overflowing, I guess, so they started
emptying them out and carting the dead bodies
into the tunnels underneath the city to store all
the old skeletons down there.

And we're not talking a hundred feet of tunnels,
not even a few hundred yards of tunnels.
There's like maybe 200 miles of tunnels
underneath the city.

And we're not talking about a few hundred
skeletons, or even thousands of skeletons.

They say there's several *millions* of skeletons that got put into those catacombs.

So like, all the walls are just lined with bones. Sometimes the people who put the skeletons in there made geometric designs with the different types of bones. This one area of the tunnels is all skulls, and another area is all just leg bones.

After my uncle showed me the pictures, I asked if he would go back there if he ever got to visit Paris again. He got an uneasy, far-away look on his face, like he was really considering my question, and he finally said, "No. No, I don't think so."

III.

Once I started thinking about bones, I couldn't believe how much we talk and mention skeleton-type stuff just about every day of our lives, not just around Halloween time or for the Day of the Dead festival, but all...the...time.

Skeleton imagery is EVERYWHERE. I dare you to see if you can go a day at school or around town without seeing some sort of picture or graphic or logo with a skull in it. Just try, you'll see what I mean. And then there's also tons of phrases and expressions about bones that we just don't even stop to think about...

For example:

-There's bonehead and numbskull when you do something stupid, such as hitting your funny bone.

-Maybe your family has a skeleton in the closet if one of your relatives is bad to the bone.

-Scary stuff is bone-chilling and spine-tingling and makes your knee-bones knock together.

-If we don't work our fingers to the bone, we won't be able to afford any food and we'll waste away to nothing but skin and bones.

-If we fall down, we might break our tailbone, and then we'd have to go to a sawbones in order for them to heal us up.

-The desert is dry as a bone, but if you get caught in a rainstorm, you'll get soaked to the bone and then chilled to the bone.

-After all of this, you might have a bone to pick with me. But I'll remind you that sticks and stones may break my bones, but words will never hurt me.

Aaaaand, that's enough. There's lots more, but for now, I'm off to bed.

Because, well, you know...

...because I'm bone-tired.

~

Ghostly Trio III: Clerihews

Edgar Allan Poe

Wrote horror, don't you know?

After workin' so hard and all that slavin',

He's famous for a raven.

Edith Wharton

Thought that ghost stories were more fun

When she wrote them in books all herself

For her shelf.

Stephen King

Writing scary stories is his thing.

A clown called Pennywise in a book called *It*

Earned him quite a bit.

~

Island Paradise

Island paradise
The tropical breeze whispers
Opportunity

~

in the library of the dead

In the library of the dead

both the books and the readers

have broken spines

~

WereCat

One thing stays the same

from human to feline
she's got
handfuls of switchblades

~

Extraterrestrial Abduction,
an Abecedarian

Aliens. Yeah, let's talk about aliens for a
minute.

Back when I was a little kid, I used to think
that aliens were neat, that they were

cool. But now I can't think of anything so
un-cool, of anything more

dumb than those grey-skinned, bulb-
headed, bug-

eyed

freaks. Always showing up in the middle of
the night to

grab people and take them up into space,
way up

high in their flying saucers and spaceships.
Then they do all kinds of

invasive experiments on them.

Just leave us alone, for gosh sake! We don't
like you and we don't want you around,
do you

know what I mean? Just go away and

leave us alone, go back to

Mars, or wherever it is that you come from!

Nobody wants to be snatched up from

out of their nice warm bed and then be

put on some cold exam table, so

quit treating us like we're your own
    personal little lab

rats.

Stop studying us like we're under a
    microscope. I think

there ought to be some sort of intergalactic
    law to protect

us from these extraterrestrial creeps who
    come and

visit our planet

whenever they want to do something crazy
    like

x-ray our brains and stuff.

Yup. I'd like to turn the tables on them. I'd
    like to give *them* a

zap with some weird rays and let them see
    how much *they* like it.

~

Birdwatching During the Pandemic

A brief glimpse of motion,

then pain.

The hummingbirds

have acquired

a taste for blood.

Birdwatching During the Pandemic

Acknowledgements

Grateful acknowledgement is made
to the places and publications
in which the following works first appeared.

- "Granite Tears on Halloween" (poem and illustration) in the *Science Fiction & Fantasy Poetry Association's 2023 Halloween Poetry Reading*
- "iRobbie" in *StarLine*
- "fingernails on hardwood" in *Eccentric Orbits 4*
- "Vegetative Unrest in Southern Mexico: A Villanelle" in *Eccentric Orbits 3*
- "Love is in the Stars: A Sonnet" illustration in the *Science Fiction & Fantasy Poetry Association's 2024 Valentines Day Poetry Reading*
- "They Say At This Time of Year" (poem and illustration) in the *Science Fiction & Fantasy Poetry Association's 2020 Halloween Poetry Reading*
- "The Autumn Forest" (graphic poem) under the title "Northern Rockies" in *Snakeskin*
- "Birdwatching During the Pandemic" (poem) in *tiny wren lit*

About the Authors

Sage Rooker writes for the middle-grade and YA markets and enjoys coding and tech and puns and the wilderness and the city and breaking barriers and breaking stereotypes and gaming and running and cooking and drawing and writing and cats and dogs and horses and dragons and ice cream. Lots and lots of ice cream.

RK Rugg writes and teaches in a New England mill town near the heart of the infamous Bridgewater Triangle. He is a Pushcart Prize nominee, an Asimov's Readers' Favorites finalist and he regularly presents at regional, national and international academic conferences on the subject of identity in speculative fiction.